Tickling Tigers

Anna Currey

BARRON'S

U.S. Edition Copyright © 1996 Barron's Educational Series, Inc.

Copyright © Anna Currey
The author and/or illustrator asserts the moral right
to be identified as the author and/or illustrator of this work.
First published in 1996 by Hodder Children's Books, a division of
Hodder Headline plc, 338 Euston Road, London NW1 3BH
This United States edition is published by arrangement with Hodder Children's Books.

All inquiries should be addressed to:
Barron's Educational Series, Inc.
250 Wireless Boulevard
Hauppauge, NY 11788-3917

(Hardcover) ISBN 0-8120-6594-8
(Paperback) ISBN 0-8120-9594-4

Library of Congress Cataloging-in-Publication Data
Currey, Anna.
    Tickling tigers / Anna Currey. — U.S. ed.
        p.   cm.
    "First published in the United Kingdom in 1996"—CIP t.p. verso.
    Summary: Hannibal, the mouse who boasts that he can do many things,
gets into real trouble when he says that he can tickle a tiger and the other
mice call his bluff.
    (Hardcover) ISBN 0-8120-6594-8   (Paperback) ISBN 0-8120-9594-4
    [1. Mice—Fiction.   2. Tigers—Fiction.]   I. Title.
PZ7.C9359Ti   1996
[E]—dc20   95-32030
                                                                          CIP
                                                                          AC

Printed in Singapore
6789 9919 987654321

Hannibal was a very fine mouse.
He was big and strong and brave and clever.
He had only one fault.

He boasted.

He boasted of how he could slip like a shadow
through jungles full of snakes,
put packs of famished wolves to flight,
dance on the backs of crocodiles
and even, he said, without turning
a whisker, tickle tigers. . .
"Go on," they said, "show us."

"All right then, I will!" said Hannibal,
and quickly wished he hadn't.

But he swaggered off with his tail held high.

And it was even easier than he thought.

Until the tiger woke up.

Grrrr...

And roared a roar so terrible that the jungle shook.

All the other tigers (two of them) came up
to see what was the matter.
"This creature woke me up,"
snarled the first tiger,
snatching at Hannibal
with his great paw.

"And now I'm going to eat him!"
"What a good idea," said the others.

"Help!" shrieked Hannibal
and took off.
The tigers chased after him.

They chased him through a jungle full of snakes.

Past a pack of famished wolves,
who fled at the sight of him.

Across a river on the backs of crocodiles.
And finally. . .

They caught up with him.

"He's very small," said the first tiger.
"Not much on him," agreed the second.
"Barely enough to go around!" said the third.
"Go around?" said the first. "What do you mean
'Go around?' He's mine, I tell you.
ALL MINE!"

"Greedy guts!" said the second.
"After all we've done for you!" growled the third.
And while they quarrelled...

Hannibal crept between their paws
and made his way home.

It would be nice to say that after his adventure
Hannibal had learned his lesson and never boasted again —

but that would not be strictly true.